A Day I'll Never Forget

A Day I'll Never Forget

by
Dana L. Cunningham, Ph.D.
Illustrated by James Eugene

A Day I'll Never Forget

Edited by Heike Curry and Erica Kennedy
Illustrated by James Eugene

ISBN-13: 978-1518847585
ISBN-10: 1518847587

Printed in the United States of America

Dedication

This book is dedicated to the youth and families who have been brave enough to share their truths with me.

Acknowledgements

Were it not for my family who instilled in me the spirit of determination, this book may have remained a seed that was never nourished. I am so thankful for them, as they have been editors, reviewers, consultants, and a constant source of encouragement throughout this process.

I also extend special thanks to:

> My editors, Heike Currie and Erica Kennedy for their thoughtful review and suggestions on the manuscript; my illustrator, James Eugene, for bringing the characters to life; Mike Major, a wonderful photographer and family friend, and the numerous friends and colleagues who provided feedback, suggestions, and support throughout this process.

I am indebted to Waterprint Design for their professionalism, responsiveness, and commitment to giving my book its wings. I also offer my deep appreciation to those of you who would politely inquire about the status of my book. Your motivation and divine inspiration were the fuel I needed to continuously move forward.

Every day on my way to school, the school bus would go by the county jail. I always wondered about the people inside. Growing up, I heard about people getting "locked up" almost every day, but I never thought that anyone in my family would end up there, especially my father.

As far back as I can remember, my Dad has always been around. Even though my parents didn't live together, I would see him all the time. We would play football, go to baseball games, and when I got good grades in school, he would take me to get an ice cream sundae.

I'll never forget the day my Dad went to jail. It was a Friday, and I was waiting for him to pick me up to take me to the park. I waited and waited, but he never came and, when I called, he never answered his phone.

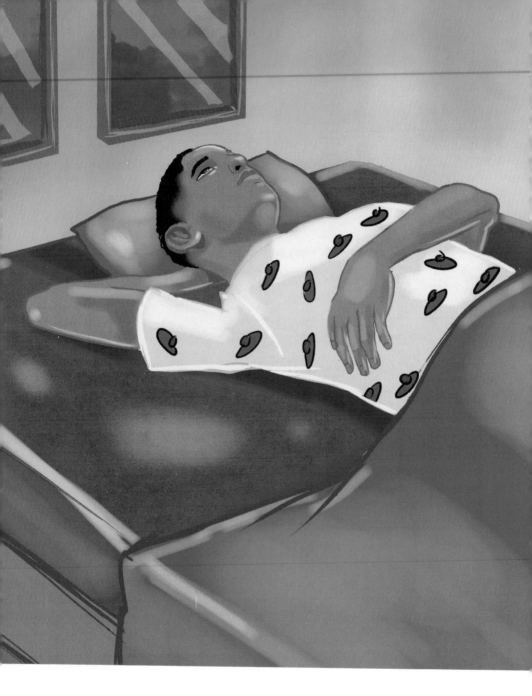

That night, when it was time to go to bed, I couldn't go to sleep because I was so worried about him. I was lying awake in bed when I heard the phone ring, and then I heard my Mom crying.

The next morning at breakfast, Mom told me that Dad went to jail the day before because he broke the law. She didn't know how long he was going to be in jail, but she said he could be there for a few months or even a few years. A few years! I couldn't believe it.

I ran into my room and slammed the door. I was so mad that I threw my baseball at the wall. Why would my Dad break the law? Why did the police take him away from me? He always taught me to do the right thing. Why didn't he?

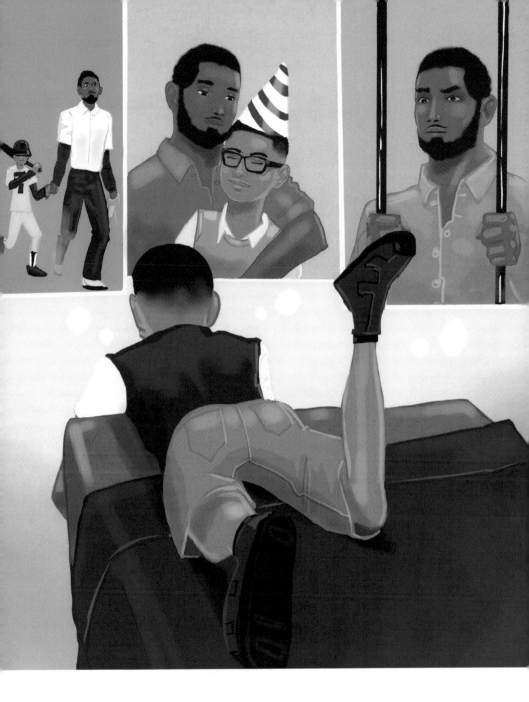

As I lay on my bed, my mind began to fill with hundreds of questions. What would I do without my Dad to take me to the park or come to my baseball games? Will my Dad be able to come to my birthday party? If he is in jail for a long time, will he forget about me? Will I be able to see him? Will my Dad get into fights and get hurt like the people in jail on TV?

I couldn't stop thinking about him and wondering about so many things. I cried myself to sleep.

On Sunday morning, I woke up to the smell of pancakes and bacon—my favorite breakfast! When we sat down to eat, Mom said, "Javon, I know you are worried about your Dad, and you're feeling sad and upset that he is in jail. It upsets me too. I know all of this may not make sense to you, so if you have any questions about what is going on, just ask me."

There was something I had been wondering about, but I was a little nervous to ask her. When I started biting my lip, which is what I do when I get scared, Mom knew that I was worried about something. She said, "Javon, you know you can always talk to me, no matter how you feel." So, I figured I might as well ask her.

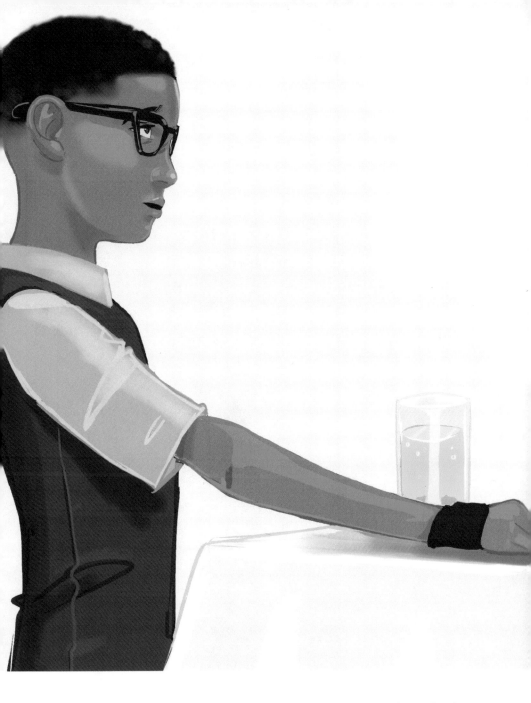

"Mom," I began, "Everybody always says that I am just like Dad. We both like to play baseball. We both love ice cream sundaes. And Grandma even says I look just like Dad did when he was my age. So, if I am just like Dad, does that mean I'll go to jail when I get older?" I was so scared of what she would say that I didn't want to look at her.

My Mom lifted my chin and said, "Baby, your Dad made a mistake, but the best of him still lives on in you. Just because he went to jail, doesn't mean that you will too. If you keep working hard in school, keep good friends around, respect other people, and make smart decisions, you will be just fine. I don't want you to worry anymore about going to jail."

Then, Mom went into the kitchen and came back with a big glass jar. She said, "Javon, you are going to make yourself sick worrying about everything. This is going to be our worry jar. Whenever we start worrying about something, we are going to write it down and put it in this jar. That way, we can get our worries out and not let them build up inside." I loved the idea!

When I woke up on Monday morning, I didn't want to get out of bed. I kept thinking about being on the bus when it drove by the jail. I wanted to stay home from school, but Mom wouldn't let me. She said she knew it might make me sad to ride by the jail that Dad was in, but that he would not want me to miss school.

To help me feel better, Mom told me to start thinking about all the fun times I had with Dad. So, when I got on the bus, I thought about playing baseball with my Dad, our trip to the zoo, making a huge snowman, and eating ice cream sundaes. I was so busy thinking of all the good times, I didn't even notice when the bus went past the jail and before I knew it, I was at school!

When I got to school, I wasn't sure if I wanted to tell anyone about my Dad. But, after sitting in class for a while, I decided I would talk to my friend, Danielle, when I saw her at lunch. I knew Danielle would understand because the police came to her house a few months ago to take her mother to jail.

When I got to the lunchroom, I saw Danielle sitting at our usual table and went to join her. I told her about my Dad and how upset I was. Danielle said she felt the same way and was always in a bad mood after her mother went to jail. She also said she worried a lot about her family having enough money to pay the bills, but her grandmother always made sure they had everything they needed.

When Danielle and I were eating, our friend, Kevin, came over to join us. Kevin heard Danielle talking about her mother, and started saying how cool it was when people went to jail. Kevin said his cousin went to jail and was able to hang out with a lot of his friends, and when he came out of jail, he got a lot of respect from people in his neighborhood.

"There isn't anything cool about being in jail!" Danielle shouted. "You don't have control over anything. Guards tell you when to wake up, when to eat, and when to take a shower. We could only see my mother on certain days of the week, and we couldn't even stay that long." I had heard all those things about jail before, too. I started wondering how my Dad was doing, and if he would want to see me.

When I got home from school, I asked my Mom when I would be able to see my Dad and she said that we could go on Saturday. At first, I was excited, but then I was kind of scared. I had never been inside a jail before.

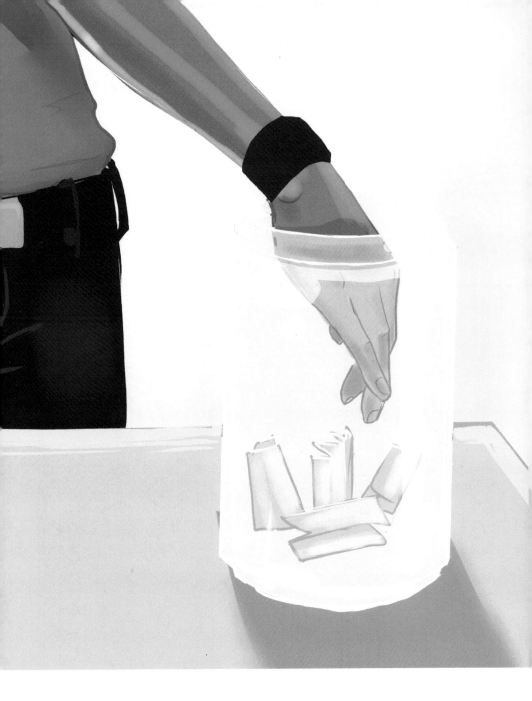

What would that be like? Would there be guards with real guns? Would I be able to give my Dad a hug or would we be separated by glass? I guess I would find out soon enough. I put my worries in the worry jar and tried to stop thinking about it.

On Friday night, I had a hard time falling asleep because I was thinking about our trip to visit my Dad. I tossed and turned in the bed most of the night until I finally fell asleep. When I woke up on Saturday, I was so excited, I could hardly wait to leave. But when my Mom and I arrived at the jail, I got nervous. Part of me didn't want to get out of the car. I started to bite my lip and my heart started beating really fast.

Once we got inside the jail, we walked through a big machine to make sure that we didn't bring any dangerous things inside. Then, a guard led us into a room that had more guards and lots of tables and chairs. As I looked around, I saw more families, and then I saw my Dad! I gave him the biggest hug ever. He said he was glad that I came to see him, but he was also ashamed that I had to come visit him in jail.

I told Dad what Kevin said about jail being a cool place. Dad said, "Javon, this is not the kind of place where you want to spend even one second of your life. Being in jail does not make you a man or bring you respect. It makes your life more difficult, and it's hard being in here away from you." My Dad started to tell me more about what it was like in jail, and he was right: It didn't sound fun at all!

I started talking with my Dad about school and my next baseball game. We had only been there about an hour when a guard came to tell us we only had five more minutes of visiting time. It seemed like we had just gotten there, and we had to leave already! I didn't even have a chance to ask my Dad why he went to jail. To be honest, I was also a little scared to ask him. But, I made a promise to myself to ask him the next time I visited.

Dad said that we could stay in touch by writing letters, and sometimes he would be able to call me, too. The guard came over again and told my Dad it was time for him to go back to his cell. I gave him another big hug goodbye, and we left. On the drive back home, I didn't talk very much to my Mom. I don't think I've ever been so happy and sad in the same day.

After visiting my Dad, I was glad to see that he was okay, but it was really hard to leave. I hoped he would get out soon. I didn't know how long we would be apart from each other, but I knew that he loved me and even though he made some mistakes, I would always love him.

Discussion Questions:

After reading this story, it may be helpful for an adult to explore the child's thoughts and feelings related to incarceration. You can use the questions below as a guide to continue further discussion with children about this topic.

1. How did you find out that your family member was arrested and/or in jail?

2. Do you know why your family member was arrested? If you do, what did you think and feel when you found out?

3. Do you ever worry about your family member being safe in jail?

4. What can you do if you start to worry or get upset that your family member is in jail?

5. Do you ever feel ashamed or guilty that your family member is in jail?

6. Have you ever been to visit someone in jail? What was it like when you went to visit?

7. How do you think your family member's life will be different once they get out of jail?

8. What do you think it is like in jail? What do you think is the most difficult about being in jail?

9. Do you think people should be sent to jail? Why or why not?

10. Do you ever worry that you may go to jail?

11. What do you think about police officers? Do you think they are good or bad? Why or why not? Do you ever get scared when you see police officers? Why or why not?